ana & andrew

Honoring Heroes

by Christine Platt
illustrated by Anuki López

Calico Kid
An Imprint of Magic Wagon
abdobooks.com

About the Author
Christine A. Platt is an author and scholar of African and African-American history. A beloved storyteller of the African diaspora, Christine enjoys writing historical fiction and non-fiction for people of all ages. You can learn more about her and her work at christineaplatt.com.

For every child, parent, caregiver and educator.
Thank you for reading Ana & Andrew! —CP

To the love of my life, for making me smile every single day. —AL

abdobooks.com

Published by Magic Wagon, a division of ABDO, PO Box 398166, Minneapolis, Minnesota 55439. Copyright © 2021 by Abdo Consulting Group, Inc. International copyrights reserved in all countries. No part of this book may be reproduced in any form without written permission from the publisher. Calico Kid™ is a trademark and logo of Magic Wagon.

Printed in the United States of America, North Mankato, Minnesota.
102020
012021

THIS BOOK CONTAINS
RECYCLED MATERIALS

Written by Christine Platt
Illustrated by Anuki López
Edited by Tyler Gieseke
Art Directed by Candice Keimig

Library of Congress Control Number: 2020941642

Publisher's Cataloging-in-Publication Data

Names: Platt, Christine, author. | López, Anuki, illustrator.
Title: Honoring heroes / by Christine Platt ; illustrated by Anuki López.
Description: Minneapolis, Minnesota : Magic Wagon, 2021. | Series: Ana & Andrew
Summary: The Lewis family visits the African American Civil War Memorial, and Papa shares photographs and facts about a family ancestor who was a Civil War drummer boy and soldier. At the memorial, the Lewises discuss how to honor their ancestor.
Identifiers: ISBN 9781532139673 (lib. bdg.) | ISBN 9781644945216 (pbk.) | ISBN 9781532139956 (ebook) | ISBN 9781098230098 (Read-to-Me ebook)
Subjects: LCSH: African American families--Juvenile fiction. | United States--History--Civil War, 1861-1865--Participation, African American--Juvenile fiction. | Families--History--Juvenile fiction. | Photographs--Juvenile fiction. | United States--History--Civil War, 1861-1865--Drummer boys--Juvenile fiction. | Soldiers--Juvenile fiction. | Ancestry--Juvenile fiction.
Classification: DDC [E]--dc23

Table of Contents

Chapter #1
Saturday Fun

Saturdays were always special at Ana and Andrew's house.

First, Mama usually made pancakes for breakfast. Afterward, Ana and Andrew practiced playing their violins. Then, it was time for a fun adventure!

Mama and Papa were always taking the family on fun adventures in their city. There were so many wonderful things to do in Washington, DC, like visit museums, tour art galleries, and see important statues.

One Saturday, after practicing the violin, Ana asked, "Where are we going this weekend?"

Papa smiled. "This weekend, we are going to a place in the city you've never been."

Ana and Andrew thought for a moment. They were pretty sure they'd been to every fun place in Washington, DC.

"Is it really here, in DC?" Andrew asked.

"Yes," Papa said. "But I wanted to finish some research before we visited."

Mama gave Papa a big hug. "And he finished last night. I am so very proud of him."

"I'm proud of him too." Andrew also gave Papa a hug.

"Me and Sissy are too," Ana said. She hugged her favorite doll, and then Papa. "Group hug!"

Their baby brother, Aaron, burped, and everyone laughed.

"Thank you," Papa said. "Now, let's get ready! We'll leave in fifteen minutes."

Ana and Andrew were excited for another Saturday adventure.

U St/African-Amer Civil War Memorial/Cardozo Station

Chapter #2
A Special Clue

Later, the Lewis family walked toward the closest Metro stop to go on the fun adventure. Ana and Andrew loved riding the local train. It was especially fun because the Metro was underground.

"Can you give us a clue?" Andrew asked. He was curious about where they were going, especially because it was somewhere they'd never been.

"Well . . ." Papa thought. "One clue is that it has to do with soldiers."

"Soldiers!" Andrew exclaimed. "Cool!"

"That *is* cool!" Ana agreed. "How about another clue?"

Papa laughed as they got to the Metro stop. He held Ana and Andrew's hands to go down the escalator.

"Hmmm," Papa said. Then he smiled. "I know a good clue. One of these soldiers' last names was Lewis."

Ana and Andrew looked at each other in surprise.

"We have a soldier in our family?" Ana asked.

"*Had* a soldier," Papa explained. "Sergeant Samuel Lewis fought in the Civil War."

"Wow!" Andrew did a wiggle dance. "In school, we learned the Civil War helped end slavery."

Ana hugged Sissy. "We had a real hero in our family!"

"That's right," Papa said. "And this is our train!" Everyone stepped into the train car and sat down.

"Now that we know about Sergeant Lewis, it is only right that we honor him," Papa continued.

Mama nodded in agreement. "And that's what we are doing today. We are visiting the African American Civil War Memorial."

She looked at Papa. "I'm so glad Papa discovered Sergeant Lewis during his genealogy research."

"What is jee-nee-AHL-uh-jee?" Ana asked.

"It's the study of your family's history," Mama explained.

Ana and Andrew were very excited. Sergeant Lewis was an actual soldier in their family! It was even more special to know he served in the war that helped end slavery.

Chapter #3
Little Drummers

Once they got off the Metro, the Lewis family had lunch at an African restaurant not far from the memorial.

"Why don't you tell Ana and Andrew a bit more about African Americans in the Civil War," Mama suggested to Papa while they ate. "That way, the memorial will be extra special."

"That's a great idea." Papa reached over to grab a large envelope he had set next to him. Ana and Andrew couldn't wait to see what was inside.

The envelope was full of Papa's research. He showed Ana and Andrew pictures of African American soldiers in old military uniforms. There were even pictures of weapons used on the battlefield.

Papa pulled out an old photograph. "And here is a picture of our ancestor, Sergeant Samuel Lewis."

Ana and Andrew looked closely at the black-and-white image. Sergeant Lewis looked very brave in his uniform.

"Wow!" Ana and Andrew said.

Papa smiled. "More than 200,000 brave African Americans served in the Civil War. And Sergeant Lewis was one of them!"

Then, Papa pulled out a picture of a colorful drum.

"Soldiers played drums in the war?" Ana asked.

"Yes, drums played an important role for soldiers," Papa explained. "Some called them Freedom Drums."

"Did soldiers like to dance to music?" Andrew asked.

Papa laughed. "Well, I am sure they did, but there wasn't much time for dancing. There were no telephones or emails like we have today.

"So, soldiers used drums to send messages. Each beat shared important information. Because the sound was so loud, messages could travel a great distance."

"That's so neat!" Andrew said.

"And guess what else?" Papa said. "Some of the drummers were only eight or nine years old! Many of the young drummers grew up to serve in the war."

Ana and Andrew smiled at each other. It was wonderful to know that children helped fight for freedom too.

Chapter #4
A March for Heroes

Everyone talked about Papa's research while walking to the memorial.

"I enjoyed seeing pictures of women cooking meals and working as nurses to help soldiers," Mama said.

"I loved learning about the Freedom Drums." Ana hugged Sissy.

"Me too," Andrew agreed. "I could have been one of the drummer boys." He marched around and pretended he was beating a drum.

"Well, guess who *was* a drummer boy?" Papa asked. "Our ancestor, Sergeant Lewis!"

"Really?" Andrew did a wiggle dance. "So cool!"

"He was one of the drummer boys who grew up to serve in the war," Papa explained. "We'll look for his name at the memorial."

Soon, they reached the African American Civil War Memorial. The large, bronze statue of several soldiers with weapons was beautiful. Part of the monument even displayed children! One was carrying a doll.

"Look!" Ana exclaimed. "It's just like Sissy!"

"Such cool uniforms!" Andrew said.

The family spent time looking at soldiers' names on the walls near the sculpture.

"We found him!" Ana and Andrew said. There on the wall was the name *Sergeant Samuel Lewis.*

"What do you think we should do to honor his service?" Mama asked.

Ana and Andrew thought for a moment.

WHO WOULD BE FREE THEMSELVES MUST STRIKE THE BLOW
BETTER EVEN DIE FREE THAN TO LIVE SLAVES

DOUGLASS MARCH 2 1863

"I think we should march around the memorial," Ana suggested.

Andrew agreed. "We can pretend to beat Freedom Drums in his honor!"

As the Lewis family marched, others who were there joined them. Ana and Andrew felt very proud to honor Sergeant Lewis and all the heroes who served in the Civil War.